BACK TO SCHOOL
with the
BERENSTAIN BEARS

W9-AHF-809

Stan & Jan Berenstain

Random House New York

The Berenstain Bears Go to School
copyright © 1978 by Berenstain Enterprises, Inc.

The Berenstain Bears' Report Card Trouble
copyright © 2002 by Berenstain Enterprises, Inc.

Cover art copyright © 2014 by Berenstain Enterprises, Inc.

All rights reserved.
Published in the United States by Random House Children's Books,
a division of Random House LLC,
a Penguin Random House Company, New York.

The stories in this collection were originally published separately in the
United States by Random House Children's Books in 1978 and 2002.

Random House and the colophon are registered trademarks
of Random House LLC.

First Time Books and the colophon are registered trademarks
of Berenstain Enterprises, Inc.

Visit us on the Web!
randomhouse.com/kids
BerenstainBears.com

Educators and librarians, for a variety of teaching tools, visit us at
RHTeachersLibrarians.com

ISBN: 978-0-375-97313-0
Library of Congress Control Number: 2013947747

Printed in the United States of America   10 9 8 7 6 5 4 3 2   First Edition

Random House Children's Books supports the First Amendment
and celebrates the right to read.

Contents

The Berenstain Bears
Go to School

When summertime ends
and the weather turns cool,
most little bears
are ready for school.....

A First Time Book®

It had been a wonderful summer for the Bear family. They had gone swimming and boating at the lake. They had picnicked in the woods, and taken many walks along sunny paths.

But now summer was just about over. There was a nip
in the air. The birds were beginning to fly south,
and the leaves on the tree house were changing colors.

One evening at supper, Brother Bear said, "I'm getting tired of summer vacation. I think I'm ready to go back to school!"

"That *is* good news," said Papa Bear. "Because school will be starting again, very soon!"

Sister Bear's ears perked up at the word *school*.

Mama Bear noticed. "As a matter of fact," she said, "Sister and I are going to meet her new teacher tomorrow."

This year Sister would be starting kindergarten. And she wasn't quite sure how she felt about it.

She liked being at home
with her mother and father . . .

her books and toys . . .

and all her friends.

"What will school be like, Mama?" she asked
at bedtime.

"You'll find out tomorrow," said Mama as she
tucked Sister in and kissed her good-night.

The next day, Mama and Sister
packed a lunch and took the long
walk down the winding dirt road
to the Bear Country School.

Handybear Gus was up on a ladder, fixing the roof.
"Hello!" said Mama. "This is Sister Bear.
She starts kindergarten next week."
"We'll be glad to have her," said Gus.
"Miss Honeybear is the kindergarten teacher.
You'll find her inside."

"Hello there!" said Miss Honeybear in a loud, jolly voice. "Come right in and look around!"

Sister thought Miss Honeybear's voice was a little scary. But she let Miss Honeybear take her hand and lead her into the kindergarten room.

What a big friendly room! It had yellow
curtains and tables and chairs that looked
just right for someone Sister's size.

"What do you *do* in kindergarten?"
Sister asked as they sat down for lunch.

"We read stories, sing songs, learn our
ABCs, paint pictures, play games, make things
out of clay, build with blocks—we do *lots*
of things!" said Miss Honeybear.

Those were all things Sister liked to do.
And she had never seen such big jars of paint . . .
or such fine blocks. There was even a whole
barrel of clay. . . .

School might be fun, after all, thought Sister
by the time she and Mama started home.

But when the big morning came, Sister began to worry again.

"Mama!" she said. "What if I don't like school? What if I just don't like it?"

Just then the big yellow school bus
pulled up to the tree house.
    "Stop worrying!" said Brother Bear.
"School is fun. You'll like it. Now
let's get going or we'll miss the bus!"
    He grabbed her hand and away they went.

Every so often the bus stopped and more bears climbed on.

Most of them were excited like Brother. But some of the smaller ones were quiet like Sister.

As more and more old friends climbed on, they got noisier and noisier . . . and the smaller ones got quieter.

The little bear who sat
next to Sister began to look
worried, so she smiled
at him and held his hand.

At last the bus arrived. The Bear Country School looked very nice. Handybear Gus had fixed the roof, and painted the trim, and cut the grass.

And Miss Honeybear's kindergarten room looked beautiful. Everything was ready!

23

Before very long, the kindergartners got noisy! Two of them wanted to play with the same dump truck. Two others wanted to look at the same book. And a whole gang of them wanted to be first to play with the blocks. What a commotion!

Suddenly a loud, jolly voice called out: "STORY TIME!" Miss Honeybear was calling the class to the book corner. *That* quieted things down.

25

After the story, Sister tried
everything. She painted a picture . . .

helped build a block city . . .

made a giant clay doughnut . . .

and looked at the books.

She ate all of her bread and honey at snack time . . .

and she fell asleep at nap time.

When she climbed off the bus with Brother at the end of the day, Sister was the excited one.

"Mama! Papa! Look what I did in school today!" she said, holding up her painting.

A few days later, the weather turned warm again, as it sometimes does in early fall.

Brother was restless at breakfast.
"I wish it was still summer vacation," he said, "so I wouldn't have to go to school today."

"Oh, come on, Brother Bear!" said Sister. "School is fun. Let's get going or we'll miss the bus!"

On the bus, all the bears were talking about the things they were going to do at school—soccer practice, science projects, music lessons—all kinds of things!

H-m-m, thought Brother. Sister Bear was right. School *is* fun!

And off they went in the big yellow bus
to the Bear Country School.

The Berenstain Bears'
REPORT CARD TROUBLE

When bears for sports
let schoolwork slide,
the report card shows parents
what students may hide.

A First Time Book®

It was report card day at Bear Country School. And there they were in their envelopes on each desk when Brother's class returned from lunch.

Most of Brother's classmates sat
right down, took their report cards out
of their envelopes, and looked at them.
But not Brother. He just sat there
and stared at the envelope.

Most of Brother's classmates were pleased with their marks. Most of them had gotten A's, B's, and a few C's.

But Brother stared at the envelope as if it were a bomb about to go off.

He picked it up and ever so slowly drew the report card out of the envelope.

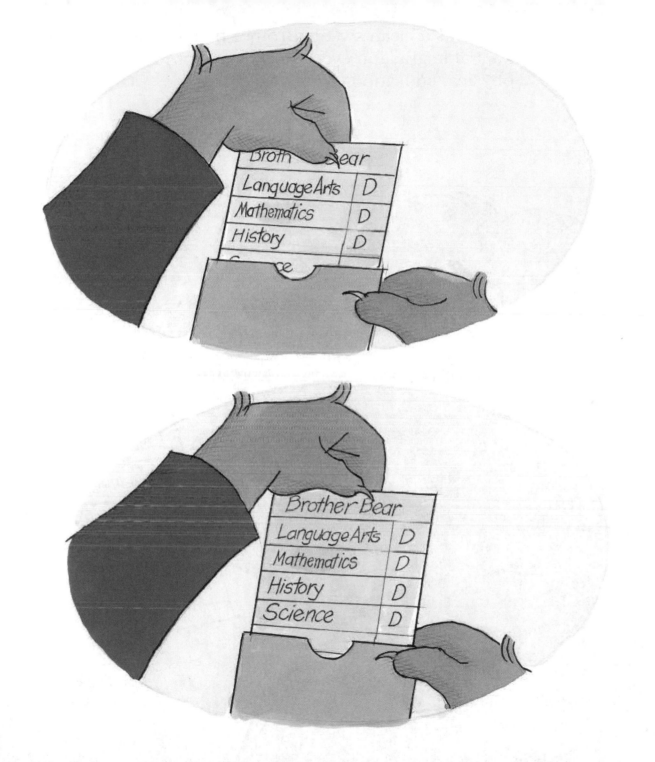

It was a clean sweep. Brother had gotten
a terrible grade in every subject except . . .
physical education!

Brother Bear	
Language Arts	D
Mathematics	D
History	D
Science	D
Physical Ed.	A

If Teacher Bob had given out A-pluses in physical education, Brother would have gotten one. That was because in addition to being captain and star goalie on the soccer team, Brother ran track, pitched baseball, and did gymnastics like a monkey.

That was the problem.

Brother was so taken up with sports that he had let his other subjects slide, slide, slide. It hadn't happened overnight and perhaps Mama and Papa should have seen it coming. But what with one thing and another, they hadn't.

And now Brother was in the soup,
deep in the soup up to his eyeballs.

Sister was waiting at the bus when school let out. She had gotten a great report card and wanted to tell Brother about it. "Brother! Brother! Guess what?" she cried. "I got three A's and two B's! The best report card I ever . . ." But she didn't finish.

She could tell from Brother's face that he must have gotten a very bad report card. He was looking straight ahead and walking like a robot. They climbed onto the bus.

"Who's your zombie friend?" asked Lizzy Bruin, Sister's best friend.

Sister mouthed, "Got . . . a . . . bad . . . report card." Sister sat with Lizzy. Brother sat across the aisle. He stared straight ahead as the bus drove away from the school.

Later, Mama and Sister watched from the next room as Papa looked at Brother's report card. Sister put her fingers in her ears to muffle the explosion. But Papa didn't explode—not at first.

Then came the biggest explosion ever heard in the tree house.

It shook the earth.

It trembled the trees.

It scared small animals into their hidey-holes.

Papa said all the things papas say when they see a really bad report card.

THIS IS THE WORST REPORT I HAVE EVER SEEN! IT'S AN OUTRAGE! A DISGRACE! TO THINK THAT ANY SON OF MINE . . .

Brother Bear	
Language Arts	D
Mathematics	D
History	D
Science	D
Physical Ed.	A
Size:	

"Well," said Papa, staring down at Brother, "what have you got to say for yourself?"

"I guess I'm grounded," said Brother.

"That's right!" roared Papa. "Grounded! Grounded, grounded, grounded! There'll be no more TV, no more video games, no more movies, no more skateboarding, no more rollerblading, no more soccer, no more sports of any kind. And furthermore—"

When Mama saw a tear forming in Brother's eye and his lip beginning to tremble, she came to his rescue.

"That will be quite enough shouting," she said. "But your father's right, Brother. You're going to be grounded until you pull your marks up."

"But that'll take forever," said Brother. "It's like being grounded for life."

"Be that as it may, that's the way it's going to be!" said Papa.

Mama watched as Brother slowly climbed the stairs and went into his room. She knew he would find in his room all the things he wasn't going to be allowed to do until he pulled his marks up: his skateboard, his rollerblades, his soccer ball, his baseball and glove, his video games, and his walls covered with pictures of sports heroes.

51

He didn't stay in his room long. He came back down again. Mama wasn't surprised. She could almost see a cloud of gloom over his head as he wandered from one room to another, a lost soul in his own house.

Papa started to turn the TV on, but Mama caught his eye and shook her head *no*. Brother noticed.

He went outside and sat on the front steps. Mama came out and sat on the steps with him. Papa and Sister watched from the inside.

"You know, it's not the end of the world, dear," said Mama.

"It may as well be," said Brother.

"All you have to do is pull your marks up," said Mama.

"By the time I pull my marks up, soccer season will be over. Since I can't do anything else, I guess I better start hitting the books." He went back into the house.

Supper that night was pretty glum. It was as if the whole house were grounded. Mama and Sister cleared the table quickly so Brother could use it to work on his studies.

"Hey, look," said Papa as he scanned the paper, "there's a pretty good movie playing at the multiplex. What do you say we take in a . . ."

But Papa didn't finish because Mama frowned and shook her head *no*. There was no way the rest of the family was going to take in a movie while Brother was home struggling with fractions and percentages.

Word that Brother was grounded got around quickly the next day. Coach Grizzmeyer was pretty disappointed when he heard about it. The team had some big soccer matches coming up and they wouldn't have much of a chance without their star goalie.

After school, Sister came into the kitchen with a long face and slumped on a chair.

"What are you moping about? You're not grounded," said Mama.

"No," said Sister, "but I may as well be. With Brother grounded, I've got nobody to do stuff with—play video games, rollerblade, practice soccer, or anything."

"You could go over to Lizzy's," suggested Mama. "She's your best friend."

"Maybe so," said Sister. "But she's not much of a rollerblader, her mother doesn't allow her to play video games, and as for soccer—forget it."

That evening, Mama took Papa aside. "My dear," she said, "I'm just as disappointed in Brother's report card as you are, but in a way we're almost as much to blame as Brother."

"We *are*?" said Papa.

"That's right," said Mama. "There's more to being a parent than cheering at soccer games. We should have been checking on his work."

"What do you think we should do?" asked Papa.

"I think he's having a hard time with fractions and percentages. You used to be a whiz at that sort of thing. Why don't you help him?"

But it turned out that Papa was pretty rusty, so Mama helped *both* of them.

Even Sister pitched in. She quizzed Brother on his new vocabulary words. The family lost track of time and got to bed late.

It was more of the same the next evening. But besides his regular homework, Brother had to make a model of the solar system. Luckily, Mama had enough fruits and vegetables on hand to do the job.

And just as they had the night before,
the whole family pitched in.

By the time Brother got home from school the next day, Papa had had enough. (It helped that Brother had gotten a B in a fractions-and-percentages quiz and an A for his solar system.) "Look," said Papa, "everybody wants me to ease up on you—your sister, your friends . . . I even had a call from your soccer coach. And I'm willing. But you've got to promise that you'll pull your grades up and that you'll never fall behind again."

"I promise," said Brother. "I don't want
to get a report card like that *ever again*."
"Good!" said Papa. "That's a big load
off my mind. Because I don't ever
want to go through being
grounded again."

"Me neither," said Sister.
"Me neither," said Mama.
"Me neither," said Brother with a big grin.